P9-CLW-818

A Sister's Wish

by Kate Jacobs

illustrated by Nancy Carpenter

Hyperion Books for Children

New York

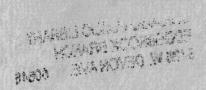

Printed in Hong Kong by South China Printing Company (1988) Ltd.

First Edition
1 3 5 7 9 10 8 6 4 2

The artwork for each picture is prepared using pastel.
This book is set in 18-point American Typewriter Light.
Designed by Joann Hill Lovinski.

Library of Congress Cataloging-in-Publication Data
Jacobs, Kate.
A sister's wish / Kate Jacobs ; illustrated by Nancy Carpenter. — 1st ed.
p.   cm.
Summary: A little girl with six brothers (including half and step) longs for a sister—though there are times when things really aren't so bad after all.
ISBN 0-7868-0138-7 (trade)—ISBN 0-7868-2112-4 (lib. bdg.)
[1. Brothers and sisters—Fiction. 2. Stories in rhyme.]
I. Carpenter, Nancy, ill. II. Title.
PZ8.3.J1375Si   1995
[E]—dc20   94-24496

For my sisters Nell and Lucy
and also my brother John.
—K. J.

For Lauren.
—N. C.

There's a bunch of kids
down on the dock
they're all catching fish
and skipping flat rocks
six boys and one girl
she looks kind of mad.

When she lives with her mom
she misses her dad
she says, "Things wouldn't be so bad
if I just had a sister."

It's time to go home
they climb up the dune
she straggles behind
she wants her own room.

These hand-me-down clothes
are ugly and worn
there's a princess's heart
beating under these thorns
she says, "Things wouldn't be so bad
if I just had a sister."

But no! She's got a half brother
and a whole brother
and a stepbrother
and oh, brother!

Things wouldn't be so bad
if she just had a sister.

She doesn't want to act tough
she doesn't want to play ball

she doesn't want to play rough
and she won't play at all.

There's a place that she goes
where a tree makes a house
and she lives in this home
with a bird and a mouse.

There's a chair where she sits
and a vase on the shelf
a fresh flower every day
she picks it herself

a book that she reads
a song that she sings

a dream that she dreams
about beautiful things
she says, "This would be perfect now
if I just had a sister."

But no! She's got a big brother
and a little brother
when she lives with her dad
she misses her mother
she says, "Things wouldn't be so bad
if I just had a sister."

One day a brother
appeared at her house

he called to the bird
and he talked to the mouse.

She thought,
"Sometimes a brother
can be kind of fun.

He can
sit down to tea
(once he puts down
his gun!)."

And sometimes a brother
can be like a friend

when he's worried or sad
or she's moving again.

She wishes that she had a sister
it's true . . .

but when a brother is funny . . .

or brave . . .
or nice . . . sometimes . . .

just being a sister will do.